SCOOBY-DOO!

NOTHING S'MORE TERRIFYING!

Darryl Taylor Kravitz - Writer
Robert Pope - Penciller
Scott McRae - Inker
Sal Cipriano - Letterer
Heroic Age - Colorist
Nachie Castro and
Harvey Richards - Editors

Spotlight

POPE
McRAE

visit us at www.abdopublishing.com

Reinforced library bound edition published in 2012 by Spotlight, a division of the ABDO Group, 8000 West 78th Street, Edina, Minnesota 55439. Spotlight produces high-quality reinforced library bound editions for schools and libraries. Published by agreement with Warner Bros.—A Time Warner Company. The stories, characters, and incidents mentioned are entirely fictional. All rights reserved. Used under authorization.

Printed in the United States of America, Melrose Park, Illinois.
052011
092011

Library of Congress Cataloging-in-Publication Data

Kravitz, Darryl Taylor.
  Scooby-Doo in Nothing s'more terrifying! / writer, Darryl Taylor Kravitz ; penciller, Robert Pope. -- Reinforced library bound ed.
      p. cm. -- (Scooby-Doo graphic novels)
   ISBN 978-1-59961-921-7
  1. Graphic novels. I. Scooby-Doo (Television program) II. Title.
III. Title: Nothing s'more terrifying!
 PZ7.7.K71Sc 2011
 741.5'973--dc22
                                                  2011001369

All Spotlight books are reinforced library bindings and manufactured in the United States of America.

SCOOBY-DOO!

Table of Contents

"Ah, Rival" 4

Velma's Monsters of the World:
THE CHENOO 12

TO ZOMBIE, OR NOT TO ZOMBIE? 16

THE COOLSVILLE CHRONICLE

MYSTERY, INC. DOES IT AGAIN!

TEEN DETECTIVES PRUNE MAD GARDENER'S PLANS!

WE DISCOVERED THROUGH CLUES THAT THE GARDEN WITCH WAS A MACHINE THAT WAS SCARING OFF THE NEIGHBORHOOD KIDS.

DR. BOTNISE WAS BREEDING MUTATED PLANTS TO START A CRIME WAVE IN FLORIST SHOPS. HE DIDN'T WANT ANYONE TO KNOW WHAT HE WAS DOING!

A FEW WEEKS LATER IN LONDON, ENGLAND.

AS PRESIDENT OF THE TEEN DETECTIVE ORGANIZATION I AM PLEASED TO ANNOUNCE THE WINNER OF THE GOLDEN MAGNIFYING GLASS AWARD TO THE TEEN DETECTIVES OF THE YEAR.

FOR THE FIRST TIME IN OUR HISTORY THERE IS A TIE BETWEEN OUR OWN *SLEUTH SISTERS CLUB* AND...

WORLD TEEN DETECTIVE ORGANIZATION

...MYSTERY, INC. A CONTEST BETWEEN THESE TWO TEAMS WILL DETERMINE THIS YEAR'S WINNER.

"Ah... Rival"

Darry Taylor Kravitz- Writer
Rober Pope- Penciller
Scott McRae- Inker
Sal Cipriano- Letterer
Heroic Age- Colorist
Nachie Castro and
Harvey Richards- Editors

ABIGAIL, WE HAVE A PROBLEM.

A FEW HOURS LATER AT SLEUTH MANOR.

MYSTERY, INC.? A TIE? THE SLEUTH SISTERS CLUB HAS WON THAT AWARD EVERY YEAR FOR THE LAST FIVE YEARS!

ABIGAIL, CALM DOWN!

MAY I REMIND YOU THAT OUR GREAT-GRANDFATHER ANGUS HELPED SHERLOCK HOLMES FIND HIS VIOLIN?

AND GRANDMOTHER HELPED TO FIND PRIME MINISTER CHURCHILL'S WIFE'S STOLEN BROOCH?

WE WILL DO WHAT WE ALWAYS DO TO MAINTAIN THE FAMILY NAME! I'M GOING TO STUDY THIS MYSTERY, INC. WHILE YOU ALERT THE REST OF OUR TEAM.

THAT DAY, MYSTERY, INC. BECOMES ABIGAIL SLEUTH'S NEW OBSESSION.

VERY INTERESTING. THIS SCOOBY-DOO IS OBSESSED WITH A TREAT CALLED "SCOOBY SNACKS."

OKAY, GANG! LET'S SHOW THEM HOW IT'S DONE!

SPECKS. YOU TAKE THE MACHINE SHOP BY THE KITCHEN, WHILE WE GO CHECK OUT THE OFFICES.

BY THE KITCHEN?

THE KITCHEN!!!

SEVERAL MINUTES LATER.

LIKE, A LITTLE FOOD BREAK ALWAYS HELPS! WE CAN'T FIND CLUES ON AN EMPTY STOMACH. LIKE, YOU CHECK THE CABINETS, SCOOB.

R'EEEE HEE HEE! RCOOBY R'ACKS!

ELSEWHERE IN THE FACTORY.

CHAMPIONS BEFORE CHALLENGERS!

I HAVE SEEN THAT PATTERN BEFORE.

THE FIRST TEST ENDS IN DEFEAT.

THE SLEUTHS HAVE FOUND *ALL* THREE CLUES. THE SCORE IS SLEUTH SISTERS CLUB *THREE*, MYSTERY, INC. *ZERO!*

WE HAVE TWO MORE TESTS. DON'T LET IT GET YOU DOWN.

THEY ARE THE BEST! THEY HAVE WON EVERY TIME FOR YEARS.

I'M NOT SO SURE.

THE NEXT DAY.

ONCE AGAIN THE SLEUTHS HAVE COME UP ON TOP. THE SCORE FOR CLUES IS SLEUTHS SIX AND MYSTERY, INC. ZERO. ONE MORE TEST REMAINS.

LATER THAT EVENING.

BOO!

BOO!

BOO!

GO BACK HOME!

LIKE MAYBE WE SHOULD LEAVE NOW BEFORE THEY GIVE US THE BOOT.

R'EAH, R'HE R'OOT.

BOOT! GANG, THE GAME *REALLY* IS AFOOT!

THE NEXT MORNING AT THE "TEEN DETECTIVE ORGANIZATION."

THIS IS A *HIGHLY* IRREGULAR REQUEST, BUT IN THE SPIRIT OF FAIR PLAY WE WILL HONOR YOUR TEAM'S REQUEST, VELMA!

BEFORE THE FINAL TEST, ONE OF THE TEAMS HAD MADE A REQUEST THAT HAS BEEN GRANTED.

WHAT IS THIS? *SNEAKERS?* I ALWAYS WEAR THE SAME SHOES!

LIKE, I LIKE VELMA'S THINKING! WHEN WE LOSE, WE CAN RUN FASTER IN SNEAKERS SO THE CROWD DOESN'T TEAR US APART.

R'EAH!

I WOULD LIKE ALL THE JUDGES TO OPEN THE DOOR FOR US. WE DON'T EVEN HAVE TO ENTER THE CASTLE TO SOLVE THIS MYSTERY!

IN THE NORTHEASTERN UNITED STATES, IT WAS BELIEVED THERE EXISTED A RACE OF ENORMOUS STONE GIANTS CALLED THE *CHENOO.*

THE CHENOO WOULD SPEND A GREAT DEAL OF THEIR TIME *BATTLING* WITH EACH OTHER, USING *TREES* FOR CLUBS, AND TOSSING *BOULDERS* AT EACH OTHER.

Velma's Monsters of the World:
THE CHENOO

John Rozum: Writer Scott Gross: Pencils
Jorge Pacheco: Inks Heroic Age: Colors Sal Cipriano: Letterer
Nachie Castro and Harvey Richards: Editors

BA DOOM

RRUUMBBLE

"THE MOUNTAINS WOULD RESOUND WITH THE THUNDEROUS NOISE OF THEIR BATTLES, ALARMING THEIR NEIGHBORS, THE *IROQUOIS.*"

SKITTLE

AARRGHH?!

LIKE, ARE YOU CRAZY?!

MOVE! NOW!

AAAHHH!

COOL IT, YOU TWO! THIS MUST BE WHERE THEY PUT *PARAPHERNALIA* FROM OLD SHOWS.

LIKE, WHAT WERE THEY *DOING?* A FRIGHT *FEST?!*

ROOK, RI'M *RUCK!* REEHEE HEE!

LIKE, HOW DID THEY *KNOW* IT WAS GOING TO BE *CANCELLED?*

OH MY *GOSH!* THIS IS THE *ANSWER!*

C'MON! WE'VE GOT TO FIND THE *OTHERS!*

LIKE, CAN I BRING MY *NEW* FRIEND?!

RE'LL *RARE* THE *ROMBIES!*